SWitcHeS and PeePS
Man's Best Friend**S**

By Sarah Giles

Birch
Books

For Sissy-Bee and Belle.

First edition 2020

ISBN 978-1-948889-03-2

Birch Books Publishing
Washington, USA

Visit us at www.birchbookspublishing.com

TABLE OF CONTENTS

Hil I'm Switches. I'm a robot. If you are a robot too, you can skip ahead to chapter 1. If you are NOT a robot, you will want to learn the facts below first (if you don't know them already):

AI – this stands for "artificial intelligence." It is what makes a machine able to think, learn, and do tasks that a human can do.

Module – a piece or part of something that has its own task to do.

Code – this word has a couple of different meanings. For robots, the word "code" means a computer program that gives us instructions.

Wi-Fi – the way a computer can connect to the internet using radio waves instead of wires.

Many of my robot parts come from an old TV. In the twentieth century, TVs looked different than they do now.

On top of the TV, there were two long rods called antennae. You could twist and bend the antennae to get the TV signal to come in clearer.

antennae

To change the channel, you would turn round dials. There were not as many channels as there are today.

And now on to my story!

channel dials

Chapter 1: Building a Buddy Bot

Peeps the cat watched her owner Max pull the tape off the mysterious box. He opened the flaps and peeked inside. A huge smile spread across his face.

Peeps did not care much what was inside. She was waiting for her chance to check out that glorious box. A good box like this would make an excellent cat fort.

Max pulled out a small black object. It was a brand-new, ready-to-program Buddy Bot Y2K robot brain. He held the object carefully and pushed the box to the side. "Here you go, Peeps. Here's a box for you," said Max.

Peeps jumped inside to claim her new fort. She thanked Max with a happy, high-pitched **"Meow!"**

As far as pet cats go, Peeps was a rather chatty one. Her adorable meows got her family's attention years ago at

the adoption
shelter.

She would say, "**Hello**,"
"**When's dinner?**" and even
sometimes, "**I love you.**"

Her family only heard
"**Mahr**," "**Meeeeeeeow**," and
"**Prrrr**."

They didn't understand cat
language. But they knew what

3

her sounds meant … most of the time.

Max carried the new robot brain out to the garage. He held it carefully. The way someone carries a birthday cake with flaming candles on top. He couldn't wait to show Dad that it was finally here.

Max and his dad had already built a robot body. It was made from stuff they found around the house.

For the robot's face, they used some parts from an old TV. They used TV dials for the eyes. The TV antennae went on the top

of its head. For the nose, they used a bright, shiny holiday bulb. Red, of course! For the body and arms, they used some old car parts. They cleaned and polished the old parts until they were shimmering silver.

To finish off their robot,

5

they added some buttons and switches to its chest plate. Dad explained that some of the very first computers had switches. You could flip them on or off as a way of telling the computer what to do.

"What should we call our robot?" Dad asked.

"I know!" answered Max. "What about 'Switches'?"

"That's perfect!" said Dad.

Chapter 2: Switches, Meet Max

"And now for the best part," Dad said. He lowered the Buddy Bot Y2K brain down inside Switches's head box.

Dad worked for a company that made AI systems. (Max wasn't exactly sure what AI stood for, even though Dad had explained it a million times. It was something about making robots act more like people.) Dad's team had worked for years building the Buddy Bot Y2K.

Before it was finished, his company had already started working on new ones. Smaller, faster, and smarter robot brains. The Buddy Bot Y2K was pushed aside and mostly forgotten. Most of the old Buddy Bots had been recycled, but not all of them.

Dad was able to rescue one from
a warehouse where his company
kept old stuff.

"Now I just need to connect the wires. Then I will send him a start command." Dad twisted the colorful wires together. He went over to his computer and typed a few words.

Suddenly Switches's eye dials began to turn. His nose began to glow bright red.

"Oooh—YES! It's working!" Dad said with a big grin. His fingers dashed around the keyboard as he entered the last bits of code. He looked up from his computer and said, "OK, Switches. What have you got to say to your new family?"

Switches's mouth hatch dropped open. Max could hardly wait to see what he would say first! But no words came. Just a loud, AWFUL mix of sounds.

BEEEEE-ooop. SCRRREEEEEEECH. UNGH-oh-UNGH. SCRREEECH,boop, BEEEEEEEP!

"Oops!" said Dad. "I forgot that the old Buddy Bot Y2K was made for connecting over a phone line. Let me just bring Switches into the twenty-first century with a couple of clicks … OK, all fixed. Now, let's get him talking!"

Dad turned to Switches and said, "Switches? Hello, Switches." But nothing happened.

Max pleaded, "Come on, Switches. WAKE UP and talk to us!"

Suddenly Dad remembered. "Oh yes! Wake up—that's it! Maxie, you're a genius! I had

forgotten the special Buddy
Bot start command is 'Good
morning'!" Dad turned to
Switches and shouted into his
earhole microphone. "Good
morning, Switches."

Switches's eye dials started
to turn again. His nose flashed
twice, and his mouth hatch
dropped open.

Max and Dad sprang to
their feet. They gave each other
a super-tight hug. Then a loud,
hand-stinging
high five.

Dad answered, "YOU are Switches. You are a Buddy Bot Y2K module. You have been built into a one-of-a-kind robot body. Made by me and your new owner, Max."

Dad pointed to Max. "Switches, meet Max," Dad said.

Switches turned toward Max. He bent his arm and held out his robot hand for a handshake. The Buddy Bot was programmed to do this whenever the "MEET" command was given.

Max reached out to shake his hand. He smiled, staring into Switches's face. Inside, he felt a

laugh-bubble in his chest when
he thought about what life
with Switches was going to be
like.

Chapter 3: What Is THAT Thing?

Peeps was relaxing in her new box fort. She rolled over, tucking each of her paws under her body. It was the perfect catnapping position. She sighed a deep, comfy breath. Her sleepy eyes began to close.

Suddenly the door to the garage flew open and startled her.

Peeps saw Max and Dad coming in with huge grins on their faces. She had seen them look happy before, but never quite *this* happy.

She couldn't fight the feeling that there was something fishy going on. And cats are almost never wrong. But it was nap time. She decided not to worry about it. She gave Max and Dad a simple, friendly greeting: a quiet meow mixed with a vibrating "**Prrrr.**"

Just as she decided to get back to her nap, she heard

18

some disturbing and unusual
sounds. She looked up and saw a
towering silvery figure stumbling
through the door.

Peeps jumped to her feet. She quickly scooted backward into the corner of her box fort.

Peeps shouted to announce that there was an intruder in the house. "**RAWH-URRRRRRRRR!**" If they knew cat language, the family would have known that "**Rawh-urrrrrrrr**" really meant "**What is THAT thing?**"

Switches stomped through the kitchen. The fur on Peeps's back twitched with every clunky footstep. The very tip of her tail whipped back and forth as she tried to figure out what was going on.

* * *

Peeps liked her life at home with her family. Sure, they were tall and loud. They had weird, rubbery skin and hardly any hair. But they petted her and brought her meals to her. She liked that.

Peeps liked doing jobs around the house. Like keeping the entryway free of yummy beetles and playing with Max. He had a mouse-shaped laser toy that shot out a dot of red light. Peeps was the only one in the house that would chase it away.

One thing Peeps did NOT like was houseguests. And here, stomping its way through HER living room—**THUNK, THUNK, THUNK**—was a big, shiny new houseguest.

Who was this stranger, and why was it here? Would she be the boss of it? Or … was it going to cause trouble for her?

Chapter 4: Switches, Meet Peeps

"**Who is this *joker*?**" Peeps meowed. Max just heard "**Mawr-ruhr.**"

Switches turned his head to look down at Peeps. "**Hmm,**" he said in cat language. "**I don't know this word 'joker.' I will ask Max.**"

He turned to Max, and this

time in human language, he asked, "**What is a joker?**"

"What?" Max said with a giggle. "Switches, what made you think of that? I guess a joker is like ... a clown."

"**Am I a joker?**" asked Switches.

"What? No." Max giggled some more. He was amused and confused at the same time.

"**That THING heard me?**" said a surprised Peeps.

"Me-WOW! And it can understand me too! This is so freaky," she said.

Switches asked Max another question. "What does 'freaky' mean?"

"It means weird. But very VERY weird," Max explained. "Switches, seriously, how are you coming up with this stuff?"

Switches raised his shiny robot arm and angled it toward the box on the floor. He pointed directly at Peeps.

"Oh, that's our cat, Peeps," Max said. "Switches, meet Peeps."

25

After hearing the "MEET" command, Switches snapped his arm back into a right angle. His fingers were flexed, ready for a handshake.

"**Oh, brother**," said Peeps. All Max heard was "**Mawr.**"

"**Are Peeps and I brothers?**" Switches asked Max.

"No, Switches," Max answered. "You and Peeps are just friends. Besides, she is a girl cat!"

Peeps didn't know what to make of all of this. There was now something in the house that could actually understand her. Was this a good thing or a bad thing?

She hopped out of her fort and glared up at the intruder. Then she spun around and threw

27

her tail into the air like a big fluffy scarf. She lifted her nose into the air and strutted out of the living room.

Switches's eye dials clicked and his antennae buzzed while he watched Peeps walk away. He studied her unusual and interesting shape.

Inside his belly can, there was a tiny spark. A new piece of

28

Buddy Bot code had just been activated: Switches had just made his very first friend.

Chapter 5: Cat Chores

Peeps looked around to make sure that Switches had left the living room. Then she returned to the safety of her box fort.

For the rest of the day, Peeps watched the family show Switches around the house. But no one in the family paid any attention to her. Why did they

even need this new thing when
they had a lovely, loyal, and
talented pet like her?

Max had
an incredible
first day with
Switches!

That night, Max did not want
to go to sleep. Dad explained
that Switches needed to recharge
too. Max was relieved that he
wouldn't miss anything, and he
went to bed.

Dad led Switches over to
the corner of the living room. He
gave Switches the Buddy Bot
sleep command. "Good night,
Switches," Dad said.

Switches's eye dials lowered.
The lights on his chest plate went
dim, and he became very still.

Peeps watched Switches
closely from inside her box
fort. The house was now dark

33

and quiet. Switches had still not moved a single bolt. Peeps guessed that Switches, like her family, was probably asleep.

Peeps felt like it was safe now, so she jumped out from her fort. She leaned back on her back legs to give her front paws a good stretch. It was time to begin her nightly routine.

First, a snack! Peeps jumped up onto the kitchen counter to see if any food had been left out. Maybe a nice muffin or scrap of soft bread. Once, there was a whole squishy sponge cake up there. Oh, man, that was a good night!

Her family didn't let her on the counter during the day. But she got up on the counter every single night. No one ever said a word about that, so she figured that they must be OK with it.

She went into the bathroom and batted at the white roll of soft paper. She kept pawing and

 pawing
until the
last sheet
dropped
to the
floor.

She knew that her family
would NOT be impressed if she
stopped before pulling down
every last bit of paper. Peeps
was no quitter!

After pulling down the
paper in both bathrooms, Peeps
liked to take a little break. A
basket of folded clothes in the
laundry room made a comfy
spot for a quick catnap.

Her family would certainly
be grateful for any cat hairs she
left behind. After all, they did not
have much hair of their own, and
it was probably difficult to stay
warm.

And finally, she rubbed
her cheeks on the tall, skinny
brushes on Mom and Dad's
bathroom counter. They were the

perfect height to smooth out her whiskers.

Surely it made the family happy to see her with perfectly groomed whiskers!

Now that Peeps had finished her nightly chores, it was bedtime.

She curled up in her trusty box fort and closed her eyes. She thought about the clunky houseguest standing in the corner of the living room. She decided that as long as he kept out of her way, he could stay … for now.

Chapter 6: Say What Now?

The next morning, Max sprang out of bed and ran to the living room. He was glad that it was not all just a fantastic dream.

"Good morning, Switches!" Max said.

Switches's red nose flashed two times, and his mouth hatch dropped open.

"Wow, that's great! How did you learn to say that?" Max asked.

"I am programmed to keep learning at all times, even during sleep mode. I don't really sleep. I just need time for my module to recharge," said Switches.

41

He continued. "**Recharging does not take as long as human sleep. I use the rest of the time to learn. Last night, before starting my sleep cycle, Dad loaded some data discs for me to study.**"

"Oh, cool. Like bedtime stories," said Max. "But what are data discs?" he asked.

Switches pointed to the bottom shelf of the TV cabinet.

On the shelf was a stack of plastic cases holding shiny silver DVDs.

"**I am not sure what it all means yet. I think I have learned a little about how humans talk to each other**," said Switches.

"Oh, hee hee." Max covered his giggle with his hand. He didn't want to hurt Switches's feelings. "I think Dad gave you his old DVD collection. I'll see if he can get you some newer information," Max said.

Chapter 7: Friendly Competition

The house was quiet, just the way Peeps liked it. She was enjoying a quiet breakfast in the quiet kitchen. Chopped chicken with rice. **"YUM!"**

Then she heard Switches stomping through the living room: **THUNK, THUNK.**

"Oy." She sighed. "**Here we**

go again."

Switches saw Peeps sitting by the refrigerator. "**Bonjour, mon amie!**" he said. "**That means 'Hello, my friend' in cat French. I know how to say hello in any language.**"

"**Show-off**," Peeps said, quietly this time. She didn't want the nosy, goody-two-feet bucket of bolts to hear her.

She turned to walk out of the kitchen and

stepped on Switches's foot along
the way. She acted as if she
didn't even realize he was there.

Peeps thought this would let Switches know how she *really* felt about him. Instead, Switches looked absolutely thrilled to have something so interesting happen to one of his feet!

Peeps didn't spend any more time worrying about the irritating houseguest. She had a schedule to keep.

It was now late morning, and there would soon be a lovely striped sunbeam on the living-room carpet. And today that sunbeam would line up perfectly over her cardboard cat fort.

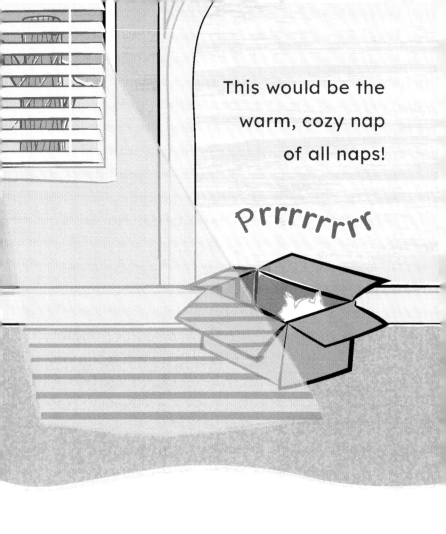

This would be the
warm, cozy nap
of all naps!

Prrrrrrr

After morning nap time,
Peeps could usually find a
human to brush her fur or

48

scratch under her chin. But today she searched every room in the house and didn't find anyone. Where was everybody? She heard noises coming from outside.

Through the tall glass door, she could see Dad, Mom, and Max sitting around the patio in a circle. Switches was standing in the center, playing some music. The family clapped along while the lights on his chest plate flashed in rhythm with the song.

"Switches, you're so talented!" Mom said with a smile.

"Yeah," said Max. "You know

how to do so much cool stuff!"

"**What a total show-off!**"
Peeps said as she watched from
inside the house.

After a few songs, the
family and Switches came back
inside. Switches followed Max

across the living room. Peeps heard a terrible *SMUSH!*

"**MY FORT!**" she shouted. Her heart sank when she saw what had happened to her fancy cat hideaway. Thanks to Switches, it was now just a stepped-on brown heap.

"**Uh-oh!**" said Switches. He picked up the heap. He tried to push the cardboard back into a square, but it was no use. His heavy feet had flattened the box, and it could no longer hold its shape.

First, Switches had barged into her perfectly quiet house.

51

Then he had stolen her family's attention away. Now he had smashed her cat fort with his big, clunky feet. This was the last straw. Someone had to do something about this robot!

The family could hear Peeps growl from the corner of the living room. "**Oh, Switches, so good at everything. Oooh! Look at all of the flashy, cool things you can do**," she said, in

a smarty-pants kind of way.

She huffed and sat frowning for a moment.

Then the edges of her mouth curled up into a sly grin.

"Let's see what everyone thinks about him when they realize what he's NOT so good at!" she thought.

Then Peeps hatched a plan. A sneaky, tricky, bad-guy plan. It was the most awful plan she had ever cooked up.

Peeps wondered if it was even a little too awful. But they say that all is fair in love and war. And this, she thought, was war!

53

Chapter 8: The Plan

That night, Max noticed that Dad hadn't come to tuck him in yet. He wandered out to the living room to see what Dad was up to. Dad was sitting next to Switches and clicking away on his laptop keyboard.

"What's up, Dad? Is Switches OK?" Max asked.

"Oh, hi, buddy. I'm just connecting Switches's brain module to our Wi-Fi. This way, he can learn by himself using the internet. And he can get newer information than he got from my old DVDs. You know, like stuff from this century," he said with a smile and a wink.

"Oh, cool. Thanks, Dad." Max yawned. "Good night."

"See you tomorrow, Maxie," said Dad, without looking up from his computer.

Later that night, Peeps waited until the last light in Mom and Dad's room went out. Then she tiptoed into the living room.

SHE was the family's perfect pet. Not Switches. And she was going to prove it! It was time to wake up Switches and put her plan into action.

How had Dad and Max done it? "**Hmmm**," Peeps thought. "**There is some sort of magic word they say. It could be anything. But they woke up Switches in the morning. Maybe it has something to do with the morning. What**

56

would I say first thing in the morning if I was a human?" she wondered.

After thinking a moment, she whispered, "**Good morning, Switches.**" Nothing happened.

"**Wait ... why am I whispering?**" she thought. "**Humans can't understand what I say, anyway!**"

So ... instead, she shouted,

Mom woke up for a moment when she heard a "**MRRREOWWW-OW-OW!**" coming from the living room. She sleepily mumbled, "Silly cat." Then she rolled over on her pillow and drifted back to sleep.

Switches's eye dials turned upward, and his nose light flashed twice.

Chapter 9:
Mouse Trap

"Hello, friend!" said Switches. "I am glad to see you! But why am I awake now instead of in my sleep cycle?"

Peeps answered, "I'm going to teach you how to do something very important, Switches. You see, you are like a pet. It's up to us pets to protect the house when the family is sleeping."

"Oh, I like to learn new things!" said Switches.

"Well, you see, there is this little red light. It lives in this mouse-shaped thingy. Every once in a while, it escapes. It's up to you and me to trap it so that it doesn't bother the family," said Peeps.

"It moves really fast, so you have to pay attention. And if you catch it, hold on tight! It is VERY good at escaping," she said.

"OK. I think I understand. Where is the red light now?" asked Switches.

"I'll check over here," Peeps said. She trotted over to a basket of cat toys on the living-room floor. She picked up the laser toy with her mouth and dropped it onto the floor by her feet.

As she had seen Max do before, she mashed the button

on the mouse's back with her fluffy paw. The button made a clicking sound. A tiny red laser-light dot appeared on the back of the couch.

Switches spun the top of his body around. As he stretched his arm to grab the red dot, he pushed all of the cushions onto the floor.

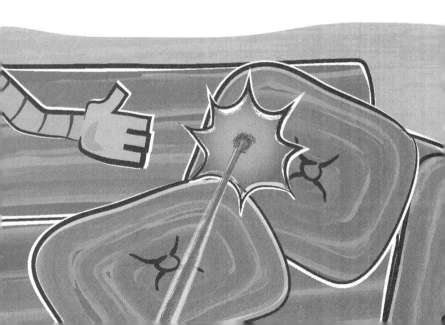

Peeps started to giggle. She nudged the mouse toy again, and the red light trailed across the side table.

Switches reached to grasp the light, bumping a stack of Dad's science magazines. They slid to the edge of the table and spilled onto the floor one by one.

Peeps looked at the mess Switches had made in the living room. Then she flopped over onto her back, laughing.

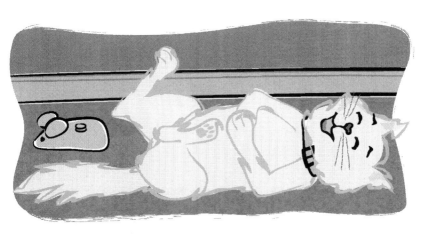

Chapter 10: MEOW-ZA!

"OK, that's enough for now," Peeps said as she rolled over to get back on her feet again. When she got up, she accidentally rolled over the laser toy, clicking it on again. The red light raced from the coffee table over to the curtains by the window.

Switches stretched his arm over to the curtains. He clamped onto them with his hand, and then YANK! He pulled them off the wall and threw them onto the floor.

"MEOW-ZA! Switches, you're so strong ... and fast!" Peeps said.

All she had planned to do was prove that Switches couldn't chase the red dot without making a *little* mess. This GIANT mess in the living room was more than she had in mind.

"Oh, man. We are going to get in so much trouble! I'd better stop this. NOW!" Peeps said.

Peeps tried to push the button and put the red dot back inside the mouse-shaped toy once and for all. She had seen

Max do it a million times, so she was sure it would be easy. But it wasn't easy. Each time she pushed the button, the red light would show up again!

As she fumbled with the mouse, the red dot traced around the living room. It moved from the window, around the wall, to the table with Mom's rare silver-dollar moon orchid.

Peeps looked up from the toy at her feet and saw Switches turn his head. She saw his eyes fixed on the table, which now had a tiny red dot in the center of it.

"**No, Switches! Switches, DON'T!**" (Poor Peeps didn't know that the Buddy Bot Y2K command she needed was "Switches, STOP.")

She shouted, "**Switches, wait! Not the—**" But it was too late. Switches reached out his left arm and swept the orchid onto the floor. He brought his other hand down on the tabletop. *SMASH!* He was so strong that

the table instantly snapped into
two pieces and fell to the floor.

Peeps heard the loud noise
of the table being struck and
darted across the room. When
she stepped off the laser mouse,
the red light finally switched off.
The poor, delicate flower lay in a
heap of crumbly black soil.

"Did I get it? Did I catch the red light?" Switches asked with an innocent, hopeful smile on his face.

"Um ... yeah, buddy. Yeah, I think you got it," Peeps said. Her smile was a nervous, guilty one.

Chapter 11: WHHAAAAT?

Click! The living room suddenly filled with light. Mom and Dad now stood at the edge of the room. They were trying to make sense of the topsy-turvy mess they saw through their sleepy eyes.

Dad stepped into the living room first, but he didn't know

what to say.

Mom, on the other hand, had so many things to say. They seemed to all be coming out at the same time.

"WHHAAAAT? What is—? Who—? How did this—?" Mom said.

Max walked in, rubbing his eyes. He stopped in his tracks when he saw the jumbled room. "Switches," he said. "Why are you awake? And WHAT happened in here?"

Peeps was hiding under the side table. She hoped that Switches was not going to tattle on her. But there was no part of

the Buddy Bot Y2K code that
would allow the robot to tell a lie.

"Peeps showed me how
to chase the red light dot,"
Switches said.

"Peeps? Showed you …
what? How would a cat show a
robot … and how did you come
out of your sleep cycle, anyway?"
said Dad, scratching his head.

Mom interrupted. "That's it! We are going to have to lock both of you in the garage at night. At least until we get this all figured out."

Peeps didn't understand the words. But when she saw Mom pointing at the garage door, she knew it was bad news. The

garage was well stocked with bugs to chase and snack

on, but it was a cold and drafty place. There were not many soft places to nap or bathe.

"Excuse me, Mom," said Switches. He was trying something he learned from Dad's data discs, called "being polite."

"Yes, Switches. What is it?" Mom said.

"If going to the garage is punishment for making a mess, then I should be the only one to go. It was me who knocked over your things, pulled the curtains down, and pushed the flower off the table," said Switches.

Switches's eye dials ticked up and down while he counted up the mistakes. **"Oh yes, and then I also smashed the table**," he said.

"So, you are saying that you did all of this by yourself?" Mom asked.

"Yes, Mom," said Switches.

"Um, you may call me Melinda," said Mom.

Switches said, **"OK, Melinda."**

78

Dad gave Switches a knowing look. Dad had made his own living-room mistakes before. Muddy footprints on the carpet. Spilled soda on the couch. Things like that. He knew that being on "Melinda" terms was a BAAAAAAD sign.

Mom turned her gaze to Peeps. "Well. OK, then. I guess you are off the hook, Peeps," she said.

Peeps could tell by Mom's face that she was one lucky cat!

For the rest of that day, the house was quiet and a bit gloomy.

Mom was hard at work, scrubbing soil out of the carpet.

Dad was flipping through the Buddy Bot Y2K manual. He

80

couldn't find anything in the instructions about a Buddy Bot

waking up by itself.

The sun dropped below the living-room window and the moon took its place. It was evening nap time but Peeps couldn't relax. No matter which side she lay on, or which paw she had on top of the other, she just couldn't get comfortable.

Was the carpet more prickly than usual, or was it maybe

something else that was bothering her?

She dropped her chin onto her feet and tried to nap. She didn't want to watch Switches being taken out of the house.

Sure, Switches was shiny and annoying. Plus he was always stealing her family away. And who could forget how he smashed her fort? But still, Switches wasn't mean.

Peeps knew that being mean is wrong. And cats are almost never wrong. Still, she wondered, had she just done something … mean?

"Aw, come on, Dad. Can't Switches stay in the house?" said Max.

"Sorry, buddy. Melinda—I mean, your mom was pretty serious about keeping him out of the house for the night," said Dad.

Dad walked Switches over to a corner of the garage. "I'm sorry about this, Switches, but we'll see you tomorrow, OK?" he said.

Dad gave him the sleep command. Switches began his nightly sleep cycle.

Chapter 12: Making It Right

Peeps couldn't sleep. She kept picturing Switches smiling innocently while he was walking out to the garage. He seemed just as happy about going to the garage as he had been about everything else.

"That goofy robot is always so happy about everything," Peeps thought. She wondered if being alone in the garage all night would be the first thing that made Switches feel something besides happiness.

"But," she told herself, "the punishment was already given. There is not a single thing I can do about it. Unless ... well, I guess there is one thing I could do." Peeps began to hatch another plan. This time it would be much less awful.

She had to hurry before

the family went to bed. Peeps jumped up onto the kitchen counter. She trotted over to a large wooden cup filled with spatulas, spoons, and other oddly shaped cooking tools.

Peeps lowered her ears. Using the top of her head, she pushed the cup of tools to the edge of the counter. She took a deep breath and gave it one last big push.

The tools rattled and clanked as they hit the floor. Certainly, this was a loud enough clatter for her family to hear from anywhere in the house.

Mom hustled into the kitchen and froze when she spotted the mess on the floor. She looked up and glared at Peeps, who was sitting proudly in the middle of the kitchen counter.

"WHAT is going on around here today?" Mom shouted in a frustrated tone. (It turned out that Mom was NOT OK with Peeps sitting on the counter at night either.)

Mom reached over and swept Peeps off her fluffy feet. She held Peeps up high so that they were looking eye to eye. "It's the garage for you too, young lady!" Mom said.

88

Chapter 13: Garage Life

Peeps was curled up in the corner of the garage on top of some old carpet scraps. She was watching a parade of ants trail from the garage door to a crumb of potato chip that had escaped from the trash can.

"Argh—this is so boring!"
she said.

Her mind wandered back
to all of the things that had
happened over the last couple
of days. She wondered why she
had been so angry at Switches in
the first place. Was he really so
awful, or was it something else?

Peeps was a cat, and cats
are almost never wrong. But in
this case, she started to think
that maybe she had been wrong
about Switches.

Switches was honest and
brave. She smiled when she
thought about how the laser

mouse had gone bonkers in the living room. Switches was kind of fun to play with too.

She thought about all of the things he had learned to do already. "**I guess he's actually pretty clever ... for a non-cat**," Peeps thought.

She looked over at Switches, who was standing in the corner, still in sleep mode. Did he even know that she was there? "**Maybe I should wake him up so that he knows**

91

he's not in here alone," she said.

"Good morning, Switches," she said.

His eye dials tilted, and his nose flashed twice. "**Hello, Peeps! I didn't expect to see you here in the garage!**" he said.

"OK, Switches. Here's the deal," Peeps said.

"I didn't ask to have a housemate, but here you are. And it looks like you're here to stay. But you've got to stop stealing my family away. I was here first, and I am the pet around here."

"**I'm not trying to steal**

anything. Stealing is bad," said Switches. "I am just trying to learn and to make the family happy."

He continued. "I'm a Buddy Bot. You're the pet. And you must be a good one, because the family said that they really love having you in the house."

"They said that?" Peeps smiled, and she felt her jealousy start to melt away.

"Well, anyway ...

I'm still mad that you smashed my fort," Peeps said.

"Oh, gosh, I'm really sorry. I hoped that I would be able to fix it," Switches said.

"All right, all right. Just watch where you are going, OK? And I guess ... well, I'm sorry too. I was trying to trick you and get you to make a mess in the living room. I didn't realize that you would be so GOOD at making a mess," she said.

"But anyway, I guess it's my fault that we're in here," Peeps admitted. She

was relieved
to see that
Switches was
still smiling.

"It's OK,
Peeps," he said.

"Now that we understand
each other, I'm going to
put you back to sleep now.
The family will be waking up
soon," said Peeps. "Good night,
Switches."

Chapter 14: Friends?

A little while later, the door to the house opened. Max came in to free the two garage prisoners. "Go get your breakfast, Peeps. I'm going to wake up Switches," said Max.

Peeps walked into the kitchen, where Mom was waiting for the coffee to brew.

"Welcome back, sweet girl," Mom said. She scooped up Peeps for a quick squeeze and kiss on the top of her head. "Now, no more jumping onto the counter!" she added.

Switches and Max walked into the kitchen together. Melinda's feelings about Switches had softened a bit since yesterday too. She became "Mom" once again. "Hi, Switches.

I'm glad to see you," she said.

After all of the madness of the last couple of days, Peeps was glad to be back in her house. She was happy to be back with her humans and with her new silver housemate too.

Switches saw Peeps sitting by the table. "**Hello, friend!**" he said.

"**Oh. Hmm,**" he said, putting his shiny metal finger up to his mouth hatch.

"**We are still friends, right?**" he asked.

"Yes, we are," said Peeps. "Good friends." The family just heard "Prrrrr."

* * *

Each night from then on, Peeps would wait until the light in Mom and Dad's room went out. Then she would wake up Switches.

He would tell her stories about what went on during the

day while she was napping.

Peeps would share her
household survival skills and cat
wisdom with him.

Then, after a couple of hours of hanging out together, Switches would go to his corner of the laundry room. (Mom did not let him sleep in the living room anymore, just in case.)

Peeps would keep him company while he connected to the Wi-Fi. Then she would whisper the sleep command, **"Good night ... friend."**

One night, just before Peeps gave the command, Switches said, **"You know, Peeps, when you woke me up to hang out every night, I only have time for a very** short sleep cycle. So I am not learning very quickly."

"Oh, that's OK," she said. "Just stick with me, kiddo. I'll teach you everything you need to know!"

You Did it! You just read More than 100 pages!

Grab your grown-up to tell them the good news! They can use this code* to download a special certificate showing that YOU are now officially a member of the

100-PAGE CLUB!

*Scan the code with a tablet or smartphone, or go to sarahgilesbooks.com/100-page-club.

Bot Talk

Human language can actually be a little tricky for robots to understand. Scientists have created a special language called ROILA (Robot Interaction Language). It is made to be easy for humans to speak and easier for robots to understand.

Cat Chat

Kittens meow to their mother to get her care and attention. But adult cats almost never meow at each other.

House cats (even adults) have learned to meow at humans to get care and attention. After all, it worked on their mothers!

Check out more **Bot Talk**, **Cat Chat** & tons of printable games puzzles and activities at sarahgilesbooks.com/activities.

ABOUT THE AUTHOR

This is a picture of Sarah Giles and her writing mate, Ruby the cat. Growing up, Sarah always had pet cats but daydreamed of one day having a robot to play with too.

When she was little, her parents gave her an old black-and-white TV that she could keep in her room. They thought she wanted to watch TV shows.

Instead, she would lie on her side and pretend that the old TV was a friendly robot. The dials looked like eyes. The large crack in the center of the plastic screen cover looked like a friendly smile.

Years later, Switches came to life in this book, and he looks a lot like that old daydream TV-robot!

TURN YOUR HEAD SIDEWAYS. CAN YOU SEE THE FACE?

DiD You KNOW ...

that Switches and Peeps's owner Max
is the star of his own book series!

Check out the Fitting Out series, for
readers ages 7-10.

Everyday elementary school problems
are not so tricky when you are an
everyday kind of kid.

But one-in-a-million Max McConk has
to find *his own* way to get through,
with a little help from science!

Made in the USA
Middletown, DE
03 October 2021

49536273R00068